Read all about it in
SMOKE

Is there any truth to the old pirate's poem?
Find out in
FORGOTTEN TREASURE

Are they tough enough to rough it?
Check out the boys who
DON'T LOOK BACK

They're burning rubber in the desert heat!
See who in
ROAD RALLY

Is the big prize worth a big risk?
Get the answer in
VIDEO QUEST

Danger lies where eagles soar. Find out why in
SOARING SUMMER

Knight makes right? See how in
KNIGHT MOVES

The chase is on — but who's hunting who?
Find out, read
DANGEROUS GAME

A family can survive anything, right?
Learn more in
SNOW TREK

ISBN 0-8114-9310-5

3 4 5 6 7 8 9 98 97

Produced by Mega-Books of New York, Inc.
Design and Art Direction by Michaelis/Carpelis Design Assoc.

Cover illustration: Simon Galkin

SNAKE RIVER

by Judy Katschke

interior illustrations by
Don Morrison

STECK-VAUGHN®
C O M P A N Y

CHAPTER ONE

"Good morning, class!" smiled the science teacher, Ms. Lund.

But so far Ms. Lund was the only one having a good morning in Room 301. It was summer vacation. The last thing Leon Williams, Pia Chong, and Anthony Grossman wanted to do was make up for their failing science grades.

Ms. Lund continued to grin as she wrote on the chalkboard with bright purple chalk.

"Welcome to our special makeup class, Appreciating Our Environment!"

Anthony leaned over to whisper to Pia. Her earphones were turned up all the way as she listened to the latest tape by Funky Girls Four. Pia lowered the music so she could hear Anthony.

"You mean welcome to an easy 'A'!" he said. Pia rolled her eyes.

Anthony leaned back in his chair and raised his hand.

"So, is this some kind of nature course?" he asked.

Before Ms. Lund could answer, Leon stood up from his seat, dropping a wad of tissues on the floor.

"Ms. Lund! I just want to let you know that I'm allergic to dust, blackberries, stinkweed, ragweed, and dandelions. Are you planning on bringing in any samples?"

At that point, the classroom door opened. In walked Mariela Gomez, looking like she had just stepped off the cover of a fashion magazine. The picture-perfect sixteen-year old strolled over to an empty desk. She sat down and began to unload bottles and jars from a vinyl bag.

"Dear," Ms. Lund said. "What are you doing?"

Mariela stared at Ms. Lund. "Well, this is a makeup class, isn't it?"

"Give me a break!" Pia groaned. She turned her music up again.

Ms. Lund forced a smile and folded her hands on her desk. "Who can tell me what this class will really cover?"

There was a long pause before Anthony's hand shot up again.

"Are we going to watch videos and learn how to recycle things we don't want?" he asked. "Like report cards?"

The class laughed.

"Very funny!" came a gruff voice from the back. The kids turned to see a tall, athletic young man sitting at the back of the class.

"Class, let me introduce you to Russell Franklin, a senior at Hayes College!" said Ms. Lund. "Russell is going to be our on-site nature guide!"

"What does that mean?" asked one of the girls nervously.

"It means that Russell will be joining you on your field trips!"

"Field trips?" gulped Mariela.

"You mean we have to go outside?" cried Leon.

"How can we appreciate our environment if we don't live in it?" asked Ms. Lund.

"My parents won't let me go!" Anthony said firmly.

"Everyone's parents were already told about this class!" Ms. Lund explained. "They have all agreed to your participation!"

Anthony sank into his chair. "Oh, man!"

Russell walked to the front of the class. He smugly folded his arms across his huge chest.

"How many of you city kids know the difference between an Atlas Moth and a Goliath Beetle?" he asked.

No hands went up. "Just as I thought!" he smirked, shaking his head.

Pia had turned down her earphones at the sight of Russell. She leaned over to Anthony. "Easy 'A,' huh?"

"On your trips, you kids will be white-water rafting down Snake River!" announced Ms. Lund. She picked up a sheet of paper. "Isn't that exciting?"

The class replied with grumbles and groans.

"And the lucky group going first will consist of . . . Anthony Grossman, Mariela Gomez, Pia Chong, and Leon Williams!"

Leon jumped up from his seat. "Dampness kicks up my sinuses!" he croaked. "And I'm allergic to almost every kind of fish—including minnows!"

Russell pointed a finger at Leon. "Saturday! Seven a.m. Bring lunch, liquids, and yourself!"

Ms. Lund looked out over her shocked class.

"Now, I know a lot of you are a little green at outdoor living . . ." she laughed.

The class nodded.

"But that's all the more reason for discovering the wonders and beauty of nature!" Ms. Lund declared. Her face was beaming. "Besides, you do want to pass science, don't you?"

The class nodded again.

"Good!" smiled Ms. Lund. "We'll discuss our field trips later."

Ms. Lund then reached behind her desk. Pia's face lit up as she saw her teacher pull out a cassette recorder.

"But until then, I have a little surprise for you all!" Ms. Lund winked.

"Yeah! Party time!" Pia whispered, whipping off her earphones.

"I'm going to play the songs of the humpback whale!" said Ms. Lund. "This is how they talk to each other!"

The class stared into space as the eerie sounds filled the room.

"Cool!" gasped Anthony. "Singing fish!"

Pia grabbed her earphones. "I think I'll stick to Funky Girls Four!"

CHAPTER TWO

The morning of the rafting trip arrived too soon for Anthony, Mariela, Leon, and Pia.

At the first sign of light, Russell was already standing in front of the school. The raft was tied down on top of the van, inflated and ready to ride.

"You're five minutes late!" Russell called to Leon as he came around the corner.

"I had to stop at the all-night drugstore for bug spray!" Leon said. Russell looked at the first-aid supplies in Leon's hands. Then he reached over for the book sticking out from Leon's backpack.

"Hmm. *Guide to Medical Symptoms*," Russell read. "Planning on feeling ill, are we?"

"I already do!" said Leon, his eyes on the raft.

They both turned to see Pia walking toward the school. She was singing along to a song on her tape player.

"You won't be needing those!" said Russell. He pointed to her earphones and her tape player.

Pia glared at Russell and gave her gum an annoying crack.

"I heard it's going to rain!" she announced as she took off her earphones.

"Where did you hear that?" demanded Russell.

"On the radio," Pia smiled wickedly. "You know, the one I was just listening to!"

"She's right!" Leon said, nodding his head. "Whenever it feels like rain, the scar on my knee starts to itch. And it's really itching now!"

"It's just fog!" insisted Russell. "When it lifts, you're going to be blinded by the sunshine!"

Pia saw Mariela crossing the street toward the school.

"Speaking of blinding, get a load of that outfit!" said Pia.

Mariela was wearing a bright jumpsuit and a flowing scarf. She was dressed more for a fashion show than a rafting trip!

"I saw this in House of Fashion magazine," Mariela said, posing proudly.

"Oh, really?" asked Pia. "I thought it was from the House of Wax!"

Mariela put her hands on her hips and glared back at Pia.

"Yo!" came a voice. "Ahoy, mates!"

Everyone turned to see Anthony coming down the block. His arm was around his girlfriend, Marci.

Russell checked off Anthony's name on the list.

"Add Marci's name to that, Russ!" beamed Anthony. "She spells it with an 'i' at the end!"

"And dot the 'i' with a heart," Marci added, reaching for the pencil.

"What are you talking about? She can't come along!" said Russell.

Anthony put his hand on Russell's shoulder and lead him off to the side.

"Listen . . . Russ," he said. "She'll be really quiet on the raft! See? She even brought a book!"

"No!" replied Russell. "Absolutely not! And the name is Russell, not Russ!"

Hearing Russell's response, Marci marched over to Anthony.

"I got up this early for nothing? Thanks a lot!" she complained.

"Oh, give me a break!" moaned Pia.

Russell gathered together the unwilling rafters. "Okay!" he boomed. "Is everyone ready for the great

outdoors?"

"It's going to rain . . . " said Pia in a sing-song voice.

Russell frowned at Pia. "Everyone into the van!" he said.

"I want a window seat!" demanded Anthony.

"I'll take any seat that's not next to her," Mariela snapped, pointing to Pia.

"Is it a long ride?" Leon asked Russell. "I get carsick!"

"No kidding!" said Russell as he slammed the door shut.

The van pulled away from the school. The group watched Marci blow kisses to Anthony. Anthony pretended to catch them. Pia shook her head in disgust.

Leon leaned over Mariela to yell out the window. "My name is Leon Williams!" he called. "And my dental records are with Doctor Marvin Fleckstone! Marvin Fleckstone!"

There was a brief silence as the van left their familiar surroundings.

Instantly bored, Anthony leaned over to Leon. "So, Leon, my man!" he said. "Who are you seeing now?"

Leon looked back. "For my allergies? Doctor Lois Rivera."

"No, man!" cried Anthony. "What girl are you seeing now? You know, as in dates!"

Leon looked at Mariela and Pia. He blushed.

"Leave him alone, Anthony!" snapped

Pia. Anthony sighed and fell back in his seat.

An hour later, the group was looking out the van's windows at trees and rolling hills.

"Pretty neat scenery, huh?" grinned Russell. "Just smell that fresh green grass!"

Leon sneezed. Anthony yawned loudly.

"Can we listen to some music?" asked Mariela.

Russell reached into the glove compartment and pulled out a cassette.

"Which one is that? The whales sing Sinatra?" joked Pia.

"Nope," Russell answered. "It's something better. It's a tape of traditional New England sea chanties! You might recognize some of them!"

"I doubt it," said Pia, sliding back into her seat.

Suddenly Mariela spotted something from her window.

"Look! she cried excitedly. "It's a red blue jay!"

"That's a cardinal," groaned Russell. He shook his head. "City kids."

CHAPTER THREE

Raindrops had dotted the windshield by the time the van reached the banks of Snake River.

The four teenagers leaned over in their seats to stare at the water. Here it was calm. But downriver, rapids were foaming and bubbling.

"The water's moving so fast down there!" Mariela said.

"That's why it's called white water!" explained Russell as he parked the van.

"So where's the blinding sun?" asked Pia.

"A little rain never hurt anyone," said Russell. "It's a fine day!"

"Maybe for the ducks!" grumbled

Anthony. The four teenagers piled out of the van.

Russell tossed out the safety equipment. They each caught a helmet and a bright yellow life jacket.

"Does this jacket come in any other color?" asked Mariela. "Neon is so eighties!"

"Now listen carefully!" said Russell, ignoring Mariela. "You'll each get one paddle, which you should hold with both hands!"

"No kidding!" smirked Pia.

"In the event we get stuck on a rock, never use your paddle to free the raft!" Russell continued.

"What do we do instead?" asked Anthony.

"We jump out and we push!" answered Russell. "And if the currents start dragging you away, float down the river with your feet up!"

"Oh, my gosh!" cried Leon. "We're going to die!"

"Are there any questions about the river itself?" asked Russell.

"Yeah!" called Anthony. "Are there any snakes in the river?"

"I have a better question," sneered Pia. "Is there more air in that raft, or in

Anthony's head?"

"Anthony's question was a good one, Pia," Russell said.

"It was?" Anthony asked, surprised.

"This river was probably named for the way it winds and snakes its way between the mountains. As for snakes, every river has its share!" explained Russell.

"I guess that means . . . yes!" gulped Mariela.

"Now, if there aren't any other

questions," said Russell, "let's do some serious rafting!"

Everyone helped drag the raft off the van except Leon. He was too busy collecting his emergency supplies and his medical book. Anthony stared angrily at the book and first-aid kit in Leon's arms.

"You're taking all that in the raft?" he demanded. "No wonder there was no room for Marci!"

"Thank goodness for that!" said Pia.

"Who would want to spend four hours in a raft with someone who dots her 'i's with little hearts? Give me a break!"

"Can we please call a cease-fire?" Russell begged as they launched the raft into the water.

After a clumsy entrance, all five of them were seated in the raft. The water was calm enough as the raft began its trip down the river.

"See?" smiled Russell. "This isn't so bad!"

"Speak for yourself!" said Mariela. "This moist air is ruining my hairdo!"

"Not to mention my sinuses!" added Leon. He sprayed his nostrils with nasal spray.

Anthony began splashing Pia with his paddle. They all could hear Russell mumbling to himself: "It's only one day. It's only one day. It's only one day . . ."

The water didn't stay quiet for long. Soon the raft was bobbing swiftly on fast-moving currents. The rain also started coming down harder.

"Why don't we pull over until the rain dies down?" suggested Russell.

Remembering her weather forecast, Pia looked back at Russell with a smug smile. "Yes! Why don't we?"

They settled down on a nearby bank, under the shelter of a big leafy tree.

"Anybody want some tofu and bean sprout sandwiches?" Russell asked.

"No thanks!" four voices answered at once. The teens began pulling out food from their backpacks.

"Donuts?! Chocolate bars?! Potato chips?!" Russell cried in horror. "When we get back, remind me to show you slides of the insides of a large intestine!"

The group made gagging sounds.

Everybody then sat around eating. When she was finished, Mariela stood up, brushed the crumbs off her jacket and walked toward the river. She carried the empty plastic box that had held her snacks.

"Where are you going?" shouted Pia.

"I read about a model who uses fresh mud as a beauty treatment! I might as well stock up!" Mariela called back.

"Sorry I asked," Pia shook her head.

Russell stood up to follow Mariela. "Some water got in the raft while we were going down the river. I'd better start bailing it out," he said.

Russell glanced at Mariela as she

stood on the riverbank scooping up mud. Suddenly his blood froze. Just a few feet away from Mariela there was a rippling in the water.

"Mariela!" he exclaimed. "Stand very still!!"

"Why?" she called back. Suddenly Mariela saw why. The blood rushed from her face. A snake was slithering toward her from the river. As Mariela turned to run, she slipped on the mud. She fell within inches of the snake. Its head was coming up out of the water.

"No!" shouted Russell. He ran toward Mariela as the snake coiled to strike. Just as Russell reached her, the snake lunged forward. Russell howled as he felt the sharp fangs of the snake dig into his ankle. The snake pulled its head back, then struck again. Russell stumbled back on the muddy riverbank. Grabbing a rock, he threw it at the snake. The snake hissed, then slithered away into the grass.

Anthony, Leon, and Pia ran toward the river.

"What's going on?" called Pia.

The four teenagers stared at Russell as he slumped over, clutching his leg.

CHAPTER FOUR

"Russell?" asked Mariela softly. "Are you okay?"

Pia frowned at Mariela. "What kind of question is that? He was bitten by a snake. It was all because of your stupid beauty treatment!"

"Maybe it was just some wimpy water snake!" suggested Anthony. He kneeled down next to Russell. "It was, wasn't it Russ?"

Russell rolled his sock down. He studied the bite. "See the shape of the bite marks?"

Anthony leaned over and wrinkled his nose.

"That tells you it was poisonous," said

Russell. His voice was shaking slightly. "It was probably a cottonmouth."

The rain was coming down more heavily now, but the group did not notice.

"What can we do to help?" asked Pia. She was beginning to panic.

Anthony turned to Leon. "Get your first-aid book! Quick!"

"Oh, now you're happy I brought it," began Leon.

"Just get it!" snapped Anthony.

While Leon ran to the raft, Russell took a deep breath and began instructions.

"Okay, listen up," he said. "Tie a band above the bite—about two to four inches up."

"Where do we get a band?" asked Anthony.

Mariela paused before pulling the colorful scarf from around her neck. "Here," she said. "Take this."

Pia grabbed it from her hand. "Well!"

she smiled. "I'm impressed!"

As Pia tied the scarf, Leon came running back with the first-aid kit and the medical book. He had already found the chapter on snake bites.

"Do they say anything about sucking out the venom?" asked Anthony. "I saw that in a movie."

"Eeeeewwwwww!" whined Mariela.

"Don't worry," said Russell. "You won't have to do that."

The group noticed that Russell was beginning to shiver.

"It could be hypothermia!" claimed Leon. He pointed to a page in the book. "That's when your body temperature begins to drop below normal." He moved his finger down the page. "The book says to feed the patient sugar!"

"No problem!" cried Anthony as all four teenagers dug into their pockets.

They watched Russell force down a jelly donut and a cola.

"Good, huh?" asked Pia.

"Terrific," moaned Russell. He looked up at the four worried faces.

"Look," he said. "My ankle is beginning to swell. I'm starting to feel dizzy. You've got to get me to a hospital. Fast."

"Sure," said Anthony. "We'll carry you through the woods. There's got to be a hospital somewhere nearby!"

"No!" Russell insisted. "I'm too heavy to carry and if I walk, the poison will spread faster. We'll have to take the raft down the river!"

"The river?" cried Leon. "In a downpour like this?"

Mariela pointed to the water crashing against the rocks. "Look at it out there! We'll never make it!"

"Yes, we will," said Russell.

By now Pia was furious. "No we won't!" she cried. "It's all your fault! You made us go rafting in this weather! Now we're all in danger!"

"Chill out, Pia," said Anthony. "If it

were you who had been bitten by the snake, Russell would help you out!"

"Yeah," agreed Leon. "Look how he saved Mariela!"

Pia kicked a rock into the river. She heard Russell moan.

"Okay!" she snapped, spinning around. "What are we waiting for?"

They helped Russell with his helmet and his life jacket. Carefully, they got

him into the middle of the raft. With Pia and Anthony in the front and Leon and Mariela in the back, they launched themselves into the river.

"How are you doing?" Mariela asked Russell.

"Kind of . . . groggy," he murmured.

"That's pretty accurate!" nodded Leon. "The book says that first you get groggy, throw up, and pass out. Then you—"

"Will you shut up?" shouted Anthony.

The rain made it difficult to see as the raft bounced over the heavy rapids. Suddenly the raft stopped short, making everyone lurch forward.

"What happened?" asked Leon.

"We're stuck on a rock!" shouted Pia. She turned to Anthony. "Didn't you see it coming?"

"It was on your side!" he shouted back.

"Here, let me try!" said Leon. He thrust his paddle in the water. He

pushed it hard against the rock.
Suddenly the paddle snapped in half.

"I told you!" groaned Russell. "Never
use a paddle to free the raft!"

"Don't say anything!" Pia called back
to Russell. "You're supposed to relax!
Just leave it to us!"

The four sat still in the raft, dazed
and confused. After a few minutes, Pia

turned to Russell.

"Okay, Russell. You win. What do we do?" she asked.

"Get out and push," he groaned. "It's not that deep here."

"Get out?" cried Leon.

"In the river?" shrieked Mariela.

"Come on," groaned Anthony. "We're soaking wet already!"

Grumbling, the four teenagers lowered themselves into the chilly waters.

"There goes this outfit!" said Mariela.

Pia stared at Mariela in disbelief.

"I was kidding, okay?" Mariela said with a playful splash. Pia smiled back.

They pushed and pulled at the raft for what seemed like forever. All of a sudden, Anthony lost his footing and slipped on the rock.

"Oh, great!" cried Anthony. He stared down at a bloody cut on his leg.

"Way to go, Anthony!" shouted Pia. "You freed the raft!"

After they all piled back into the raft, Anthony reached for a roll of bandages from Leon's first-aid kit.

"My kit came in pretty handy, didn't it?" beamed Leon.

"You won't let me forget it, will you?" grinned Anthony.

The wind was blowing heavily by the time the raft entered the narrowest stretch of the river. A short distance away, they could see a huge tree bending over.

"Oh, my gosh!" screamed Mariela. "We can't go under that! It'll fall right on top of us!"

"We have to!" Anthony screamed back. "This raft has a mind of its own!"

"Here we go!" shouted Pia.

Holding their breaths, the team used the oars to guide the raft under the cracking tree.

The raft had barely passed through when they heard a loud snap. The group turned around and watched the tree fall into the river.

"We made it!" gasped Leon.

"We are the coolest!" yelled Pia.

Everyone cheered, except for Mariela.

"Hey, listen you guys!" she called out. "What's that noise?"

CHAPTER FIVE

The sound of rushing water roared louder and louder as the raft bobbed upon the currents.

"What is that roaring?" demanded Anthony.

"It sounds like rough rapids coming up," Russell said feebly.

"Rough rapids?!?" the foursome screamed.

"How rough?" cried Leon.

"Man, I can't believe this!" shouted Pia.

"Come on, you can do it," Russell urged the group.

The raft approached the rapids and swayed from side to side.

Mariela held onto Russell as the raft plunged down through a rush of raging white water. Huge waves swept them up and carried them down again. Then, as quickly as they had come, the rapids died down into calmer waters.

"Hey! That was fun!" gasped Anthony with excitement. "It was like a roller coaster!"

"Just delightful!" groaned Pia. "And all this water that got in the raft is a barrel of laughs, too, right?"

"How are we going to get the water out?" asked Leon.

Pia thought for a moment. "Mariela, do you still have that container you were going to use for the mud?" Pia asked.

"Yes. Why?" Mariela replied.

"Bail out!" Pia ordered.

"I don't see why they call this course 'Appreciating Our Environment,'" Mariela snapped. She began to scoop the water from the raft. "Does anyone here appreciate our environment right

now? I don't think so!"

It seemed as though the rain would never let up. Russell had passed out and there was no trace of a landing in sight.

"My arms are killing me!" cried Leon. "I can't paddle another minute longer!"

"Wait!" cried Pia. "There's a sign on the left bank! What does it say?"

"'Quincy Landing—One Mile!'" read Anthony happily. "We're heading for the home stretch, you guys!"

But just when they thought they'd been through it all, their raft came to another grinding halt.

"Did we hit another rock?" asked Mariela.

Anthony leaned over and looked into the water. "More like a dead tree stump!" he said. "This is just great!"

Water from the rapids was spilling into the back of the raft. The four rafters couldn't bail it out fast enough.

"Oh, no!" Anthony shouted. Look behind us!"

Coming straight at them was the large tree that had almost fallen on the raft before.

"Abandon ship!!" screamed Pia. She and Anthony eased Russell into the water and jumped in after him.

Frantic, Leon turned to Mariela. "I never got to tell you this, but I've always had a major crush on you!"

With that, Leon and Mariela plunged into the moving water.

Anthony was the first of the crew to come back up. Then he grabbed Russell by his life jacket. He swam with his arm around Russell to the nearest riverbank.

Mariela and Pia managed to swim to

a nearby rock. They watched the tree crash against the raft then float downriver.

The girls swam back to the raft.

"Where's Leon?" Pia asked Mariela as they climbed in.

Mariela screamed in horror. Leon was thrashing in the water by the raft. He gasped for air as the currents beat against him.

"His foot is stuck in one of the stump roots under the raft!" Mariela shouted as she jumped out of the raft.

Pia chewed nervously on her nails as Mariela worked to loosen Leon from the branch. Finally his foot was freed and he and Mariela climbed back into the raft.

"I can't believe you had a crush on me!" said Mariela as Leon spit out water. "That is so sweet!"

Although the raft was still stuck on the dead tree stump, they were happy to be safe.

Pia called to Anthony, who was resting on the bank. "Great! We only have one paddle!"

Just then she spotted another one floating in the water nearby. "I'm going to make a swim for it!" she announced. And she jumped in.

"Be careful!" yelled Anthony.

Pia swam a few feet after the paddle. Suddenly a strong current took hold of her. The other rafters watched with dread as the raging water carried Pia away.

CHAPTER SIX

The fierce waters were sweeping Pia down Snake River. Mariela turned to see Anthony running along the riverbank.

"Where are you going?" she shouted to him.

"To help her!" Anthony shouted back as he ran. The mud was slippery. Anthony held onto overhanging tree branches as he made his way along the riverbank.

His eyes followed Pia, bobbing up and down in the water.

Anthony remembered Russell's earlier advice. He shouted to Pia: "Keep your feet up!"

Pia did as he said. Then she managed to escape from the current by wrapping herself around a rock.

"Hold on!" Anthony called.

"I can't!" Pia cried. The water crashed against her.

Thinking fast, Anthony saw the branch of a dead tree over his head. He reached up and snapped it off.

"Grab this!" he yelled. He held the branch out over the water.

As Anthony leaned forward to move the branch closer to Pia, he felt himself begin to fall. He reached for the branch of another tree just in time.

Finally Pia grabbed the dead branch. Anthony slowly pulled her in.

"Are you okay?" Anthony asked.

Pia sat down on the bank, exhausted. "Yeah," she wheezed. "Look, about my calling you an airhead . . ."

"Forget it!" smiled Anthony. He helped her up.

Freeing the raft from the dead tree stump was no easy job, but the group finally managed to do it. By the time they got Russell back in the raft, he was conscious again. But the swelling and pain had gotten worse. They had to move fast.

The raft moved downriver a few more yards. Leon spotted the floating paddle. He leaned over and reached for it.

"Piece of cake!" he grinned, holding up the paddle.

"That's easy for you to say!" laughed Pia.

The crew paddled for a few more minutes. Finally they saw the landing in the distance.

"We made it!" screamed Leon happily.

"All right!" shouted Pia. "We are totally cool!!"

"Oh yeah?" asked Anthony. "Then how come we're losing control of the raft?"

No sooner had Anthony asked the question then the raft began spinning towards a large rock in the middle of the river.

"Feels like . . . a whirlpool," Russell whispered. Sweat mixed with the rain poured down his face.

"Whirlpool?" screamed Pia. "It feels more like the Bermuda Triangle!!"

"If I don't get an 'A' in this class . . ." Anthony groaned.

The whirlpool held the raft trapped against the rock. The foursome tried to free the raft, but they could not release it from the pool's grip.

Anthony, Mariela, and Pia struggled with the raft. Seeing another rock sticking out from the water, Leon had an idea.

"If I jump over to that rock over there," he said, "you can throw me a rope and I'll tow the raft out of this mess!"

"Don't!" cried Mariela. "You'll never make it!"

"Watch me!" Leon shouted as he stood up in the raft. He made a flying leap, barely making it onto the rock.

Anthony tossed Leon the rope that was attached to the raft. Leon caught it and pulled the raft out of the stubborn whirlpool.

"Are you sure you're the same guy whose scar was itching a few hours ago?" Pia asked Leon as she carefully

helped him into the raft.

"What scar?" shrugged Leon. He flashed a smile.

The raft floated on.

Worn out, wet, and cold, the group

finally paddled the last few feet to Quincy Landing. The four teenagers dragged Russell and the raft onto the muddy bank. Then they spotted a cabin.

"There's a light on!" shouted Pia.

She raced to the door. It was open. Inside, Pia saw a man behind a messy desk. He turned from the bowling match on his small black-and-white television to stare at Pia.

"What happened to you?" asked the man.

"Just call an ambulance, sir!" cried Pia. "Please!"

* * *

* * *

It was early evening. Pia, Anthony, Mariela, and Leon were sipping hot tea in Russell's hospital room. Russell lay in bed, propped up with pillows.

Anthony stared at the bottle hanging above the bed. A tube ran from the bottle to Russell's arm. "What's that stuff dripping into your arm?" he asked.

"It's a special drug to fight off snake poison," answered Russell weakly.

Leon flipped through his first-aid book. "It's probably a mixture of snake venom and . . ."

"Spare us the gross details!" begged Pia. She reached over and snapped his book shut.

"How did Leon ever fail science?" wondered Mariela.

"Which brings me to my next question, Russ!" said Anthony. "Did we pass?"

"Pass?" Russell laughed lightly. "After what you guys did, you can teach the

next summer's course!"

Four hands went up to give high-fives.

"Remind me," Russell went on, "never to overlook the 'natural' powers of city kids!"

"Or our junk food!" added Mariela.

"I just hope this doesn't turn you off to the great outdoors," said Russell.

"Are you kidding?" cried Leon. "My sinuses are clear for the first time in years!"

"Yeah," added Mariela. "That trip was better than ten aerobic classes!"

"Why don't we appreciate our environment again next Saturday?" suggested Pia.

"I have a better idea," Anthony chimed in. "Why don't we just appreciate a nice nature video instead?"

"Are you trying to slither your way out of another nature trip down Snake River?" joked Leon.

Everyone laughed.

"Naturally!" grinned Anthony.